Heather Butler has taught at primary level for over 24 years, with a particular emphasis on special needs, and has been involved with the teaching and nurturing of children within the local church for over 20 years. She now teaches part-time, leads story-writing workshops in primary schools and is involved with several charities working with traumatized children across the world. She is author of Stories to make you think *and* More stories to make you think, *and the section for the classroom in* Out of the Toybox, *all published by BRF.*

Text copyright © Heather Butler 2004
Illustrations copyright © Simon Smith 2004
The author asserts the moral right
to be identified as the author of this work

Published by
The Bible Reading Fellowship
First Floor, Elsfield Hall
15–17 Elsfield Way, Oxford OX2 8FG

ISBN 1 84101 202 5
First published 2004
10 9 8 7 6 5 4 3 2 1 0

Acknowledgments
Unless otherwise stated, scripture quotations are taken from the
Contemporary English Version of the Bible published by HarperCollins
Publishers, copyright © 1991, 1992, 1995 American Bible Society.

A catalogue record for this book is available from the British Library

Printed and bound in Great Britain by
Bookmarque, Croydon

Further Stories to make you think

Heather Butler

Helping children develop moral values through storytelling

Thank you...
to Pat Lewis and Eileen Littler for all your
encouragement, and to the children of Manor Farm
Community Junior School, Hazlemere, Bucks for
your comments. As always, they were very honest.

Contents

Introduction

This is the third in a series of books designed to address a range of topical and often sensitive issues relevant to the lives of children aged 6–10. It can be used on a one-to-one basis with the individual child, in a group or with a whole class, particularly during Circle Time or PSHE.

Each chapter follows the same format and includes:

- Introductory Bible verse(s) designed to link Christian teaching into the issue illustrated by the story.
- Non-statutory guideline links for PSHE at key stages 1 and 2.
- The story itself. Some of the stories are based on real-life incidents, some use a fairytale genre. Each one includes pauses in the text to provide thinking time for reflective thought, with suggested questions to encourage discussion. The stories and suggested questions have both been used with groups of children and some of their comments are included in the text.
- Other things children said which have not been included in the main text.
- Thinking time questions.
- Prayers for use in a Christian context.
- Suggested activities designed to extend the thinking time.

Fairness

Please make me wise and teach me the difference
between right and wrong.

1 Kings 3:9a

Everywhere on earth I saw violence and injustice
instead of fairness and justice.

Ecclesiastes 3:16

Key Stage link

KS1: 1a: To recognize what they like or dislike, what is fair or unfair, and what is right or wrong.

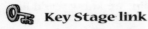 **Bible link**

Children have strong views about likes and dislikes, fairness and what is right and wrong. The Bible teaches that, in God's eyes, everyone is equal and should be treated fairly by others. The princess in this story encounters things she dislikes and feels are unfair. As you might expect, she expresses her thoughts. The story finishes with an invitation for the children to write their own ending.

The dragon with too much fire

There was once a beautiful princess who lived in a castle where half the walls had fallen down and the moat flooded whenever it rained. The dragon, who went by the name of Hamlet, had stopped breathing fire and become the princess's pet. Everything was wonderful and happy until one day when the princess's father said between mouthfuls of spaghetti bolognaise and chips, 'This castle is falling down too much. It is too old, too draughty and too big. Your mother and I have decided we are going to move.'

The princess gasped. 'Where are we moving to?' she asked in a dramatic voice. Her voice was trembling because a terrible thought was crawling across her brain. You see, every castle had its own dragon and, if they moved, Hamlet would have to stay in *this* castle, even though it was falling down. That would be unbearable.

'Now don't go getting upset, my little princess,' the queen soothed. 'We've found a nice castle that has just been built and it's only on the other side of the mountain. We know you'll like it when you see it.'

The beautiful princess could stand it no longer. 'You don't understand,' she sobbed. Fleeing from the table, she ran across the courtyard to the tower, threw open the door and raced up the spiral staircase to her bedroom. Hamlet was there, gazing out of the window at the buttercups swaying in the gentle breeze.

'Nice day today,' he breathed. 'Fancy a ride later on?'

'Oh Hamlet,' the beautiful princess gasped, 'the royal mummy and daddy have said they want to move, and if we do you have to stay here in this castle, and there is no way I am

going to leave you behind for you are my dearest dragon and my most perfect pet and I am not going to move even if they send the royal guards to make me!'

Hamlet lowered his neck and stared at her through sad eyes.

'Where do they want to move to?' he asked slowly.

'The new castle on the other side of the mountain.'

'Nice castle,' he breathed. 'I flew over it the other day. Indoor swimming-pool with bright orange slides, six bedrooms with fitted wardrobes, large moat with ducks already on it, private cinema, central heating. You'll like it.'

'But I won't if you're not there, Hamlet.'

'Who says I won't be there?'

'Because this is your castle. You were specially made for it and will die if you leave it.'

Hamlet frowned. What the princess had said was true, but there were ways round it.

'Come on,' he said, 'hop on my back. Let's go and have a look at the new castle. You never know what might happen.'

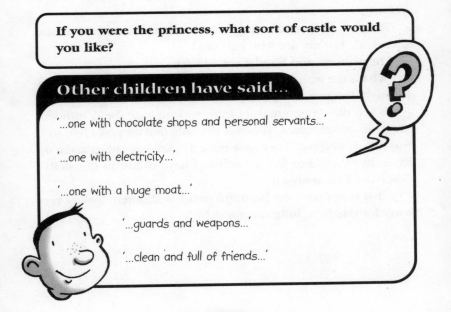

If you were the princess, what sort of castle would you like?

Other children have said...

'...one with chocolate shops and personal servants...'

'...one with electricity...'

'...one with a huge moat...'

'...guards and weapons...'

'...clean and full of friends...'

It was indeed a fantastic castle. The walls weren't falling down and the roof tiles were all different colours. Better still, the windows were double-glazed so the winds wouldn't come howling into all the rooms.

'So where's this castle's dragon?' Hamlet shouted as they circled above it. 'It must have one or it's not a proper castle. I'll give that dragon a shout and tell it it's got visitors. Cover your ears up... I'm about to shout!'

Even Hamlet, with all his hundreds and hundreds of years of experience, did not expect what happened next. For out of the well in the middle of the courtyard there suddenly shot a ball of fire, about five metres long, spinning and twisting and making a terrible racket. Through the flames could be seen a little dragon with a bluey-grey body, pointed spikes and horns.

'Wow!' the princess gasped, grabbing hold of Hamlet's back to steady herself as Hamlet opened his wings wide to shield her from the fiery blast.

'Sure is some dragon,' he gulped. 'Oi! You! Come and say "hello" and put your fire away. I don't want my wings turned into toast.'

The new castle's little dragon hovered near them. 'Sorry,' she squeaked, 'but my fire won't go out.'

The princess and Hamlet stared back.

'What's the matter with your voice?' Hamlet asked, trying not to laugh. Dragons did not squeak. They roared.

'When the dragon makers were making me,' she continued, 'they ran out of voices. This was the only one they had left, so it was this or nothing. They gave me extra fire instead to make up for it, but that's not funny because I have to live in the well— otherwise I burn myself.'

'That is not fair!' the beautiful princess shouted, feeling very sorry for this poor little dragon.

When someone says something is not fair, what do they mean?

'...that it shouldn't have happened...'

'...someone is doing something wrong...'

'...something's got to be changed...'

'...someone got a privilege when they've done nothing...'

'...they haven't got their own way...'

'...your friends do something but you don't...'

Hamlet was so sad for the little dragon that he let out an almighty roar.

'I'll never be able to do that,' the little dragon squeaked in her high-pitched voice, and the beautiful princess noticed a tear on her scaly face. The tear only lasted a few seconds before the flames reduced it to nothing.

'She's like a flying bonfire,' Hamlet thought. 'She'd be great for having a barbeque on.'

What other things could the little dragon be useful for?

Other children have said...

'...central heating...'

'...on fireworks night...'

'...showing planes where to go...'

Would it be right to ask her to do those things?

Other children have said...

'...she might fly away and never come back. Then she would be homeless because she belongs to a castle...'

'...not if she didn't like it...'

'...no, she would get upset...'

'We are going to have to do something to help you,' the beautiful princess said kindly.

'Oh!' squeaked the little dragon. 'I'm sorry, but I'm going to have to go back to the well. My claws are beginning to melt.' And with that, she plummeted back down the well she had shot out of two minutes earlier.

'That poor dragon!' the princess sighed. 'We have got to help her.'

❖

That night, the princess lay in bed. Hamlet was snoring on the other side of her room. It was just as the old owl was hooting outside her bedroom window that a thought blew into the princess's brain. It made her jump out of bed and shake Hamlet's ears.

'Hamlet, wake up!'

'Eeehg!'

'Wake up! Tell me something. Years ago, you used to breathe fire, didn't you?'

'Eeehg!'

'Then you stopped breathing fire. Tell me. How did you stop?'

'It was so long ago, I can hardly remember. Let me think... oh yes, I remember...'

Hamlet went pink all over and looked at the floor. 'I... I... fell in love,' he whispered.

'You fell in love! Who with?'

'That would be telling.'

'Well, tell. Now!'

Hamlet stretched his neck out and rested it across the floor.

'She was the most gorgeous dragon I've ever seen,' he said sadly. 'Very beautiful, with an ice-cold tail. Only she fell in love with George, the dragon from a castle 500 miles away, and married him instead of me. It was all a long time ago and I'd rather not talk about it.'

'You never told me that before,' the beautiful princess said, and she put her arms round Hamlet's shoulders and hugged him.

'You never asked.'

'And your fire went out when you fell in love?'

Hamlet nodded. 'You can't kiss someone if you're breathing fire over them, can you?'

The princess thought about that one. Hamlet was right.

'But what happened when they got married? She couldn't leave her castle and neither could George.'

'Oh no. There's an ancient law that says if two dragons get married, one of them is allowed to leave their castle.'

'That's simple, then,' the beautiful princess smiled. 'After all, this is a fairytale and who knows what might happen!'

Other things children have said

'...it's horrible when something isn't fair...'

'...you have to learn what is right and what is wrong. You learn that off your parents and your teacher and sometimes your friends...'

'...people who believe in God learn what is right from God...'

Thinking time

- What do you think the word 'fair' means?
- How do you make sure what you do is fair when:

  ...you're watching television with someone else?

…you're playing in the playground?

…you want to talk to your teacher but someone else is ahead of you?

…a friend falls over when you are in the middle of a game?

Prayer

Dear God, it's hard to always be fair. Help me to have the courage to make sure everyone is treated the same. Amen

Thinking time activity

Write your own ending to the story, giving it:

a. An ending that is fair (or unfair) to both of the dragons.

b. An ending where the king does something that is wrong (or right).

c. An ending where the beautiful princess, Hamlet or the little dragon do something they like (or dislike) doing.

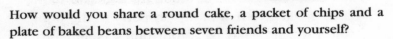

How would you share a round cake, a packet of chips and a plate of baked beans between seven friends and yourself?

Making mistakes

Be generous, and some day you will be rewarded.
Share what you have with... others, because you never
know when disaster may strike.

Ecclesiastes 11:1–2

Later that day Zacchaeus stood up and said to the
Lord, 'I will give half of my property to the poor.
And I will now pay back four times as much to
everyone I have ever cheated.'

Luke 19:8

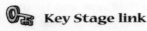
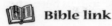 **Bible link**

Mistakes are sometimes deliberate, sometimes accidental. Occasionally we can make up for them; sometimes we can't. There is a story in the Bible about Zacchaeus, a tax collector who became rich by cheating. After spending time with Jesus, he realized he was wrong and wanted to make amends for his mistakes. In the story, Kristie finds that it's not always an easy thing to do.

Chocolate biscuits

Kristie was hungry. As it happened, she had four of her favourite chocolate biscuits in her bag. She could almost taste them as she sat under the willow tree watching the others dragging a branch across the grass.

It was the summer holidays and they were building a den at the bottom of Justine's enormous garden. The plan was to sleep in the den tonight if it didn't rain.

'Mum doesn't want us in the kitchen because she's got some friends coming round, so bring your lunch with you,' Justine had said on the phone. 'And your sleeping bag.'

So here they were, building a den under the big old tree with its overhanging branches. They had found an old piece of carpet in Justine's garage and then some cardboard boxes which were like little cupboards. Only now, Kristie was hungry, and she could picture those four chocolate biscuits lying in the bottom of her bag—her favourites.

'There's one for each of you,' Mum had said as they packed

her lunch in her bag. But if Kristie sneaked off now and ate one without telling the others, they would never know what they had missed and she could have all four to herself.

She stood up and helped the others push the branch into place, filling in the gap between the ground and where the willow had been cut back.

'I need to go to the loo,' she said. The outside loo was by the swimming-pool and that was where their bags were.

'Well, while you're gone we'll drag that other branch across,' Asha said. 'It's nearly finished then.'

As soon as Kristie reached the swimming-pool, she went straight to her lunchbox, pulled out the packet of biscuits, ripped off the cellophane cover, then the green wrapper, and sank her teeth into the soft white chocolate. That tasted so good! Why should she share them with the others?

Would Kristie's decision affect her friends in any way?

Other children have said...

'...her friends might fall out with her if they knew she wasn't sharing...'

'...if her mum found out she'd get in big trouble...'

'...in a way, it's stealing from your friends, even though they don't know about it...'

'...they wouldn't trust her any more if they knew what she'd done...'

'...no—her friends would never find out...'

When she returned, the others were sitting on the carpet inside the den.

'We don't need to do much more,' Asha was saying, 'and there's loads of room. Let's go and get our sleeping bags. That'll make it even more comfortable.'

'I'm hungry,' Karen said a few minutes later.

'And me,' Asha agreed.

'But it's only eleven o'clock,' Kristie said. She, of course, wasn't hungry any more.

The others decided to have their lunch anyway, so they all went to the swimming-pool and sat on the plastic chairs round the table next to the barbeque.

'I've got cheese sandwiches,' Karen sighed. 'I'm bored with cheese.'

'I've got egg,' Asha added.

'Let's share them all, then,' Justine said. 'There are some plates in that box. Mum uses them when we have a barbecue. We can put all our sandwiches on one of them, and I've got four cakes. Mum said it was one for each of us.'

They all watched as she laid four huge cream doughnuts on a dark blue plate.

'My mum gave me four packets of sweets,' Karen said and added them.

'And mine gave me a huge packet of crisps,' Asha said, opening it.

'My mum's only given me sandwiches, an apple and a yoghurt,' muttered Kristie.

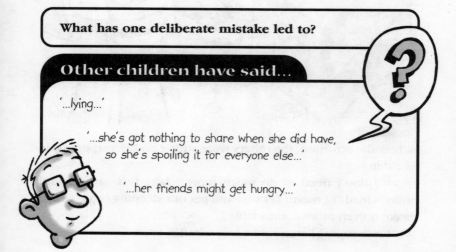

What has one deliberate mistake led to?

Other children have said...

'...lying...'

'...she's got nothing to share when she did have, so she's spoiling it for everyone else...'

'...her friends might get hungry...'

Kristie felt a bit awkward as she reached out for a cream doughnut. Maybe she should have put the three remaining chocolate biscuits out anyway. They could have halved them or something, but it was too late now. They were in her bag lying on the floor next to her.

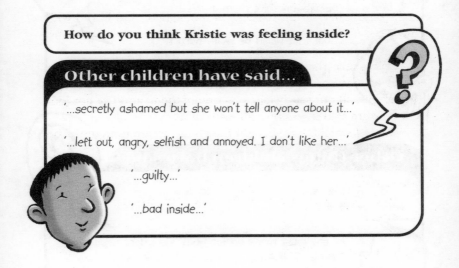

How do you think Kristie was feeling inside?

Other children have said...

'...secretly ashamed but she won't tell anyone about it...'

'...left out, angry, selfish and annoyed. I don't like her...'

'...guilty...'

'...bad inside...'

The cream from the doughnuts dribbled over Karen's right hand. She licked it.

'It's all sticky!' she laughed.

'Go and wash in the swimming-pool, then,' Justine said.

Karen stood up and, as she did so, two muddy shoes landed on Kristie's bag, followed by a crunching noise. Those biscuits were well and truly squashed, but Kristie could say nothing about it.

After lunch, Asha wanted to go for a walk to the shops up the road. It would pass the time until Justine's mum's friends had gone. They could go in the pool then. Justine's mum insisted on being there to watch them. As they walked along the road, Kristie knew she had some money Mum had given her to spend on whatever she liked.

What should Kristie do?

'...buy some biscuits and give them away...'

'...but that would be really hard to do...'

'...buy them and tell her friends what she did...'

Other things children have said

'... if they were real friends, they would help her learn how to share...'

'...she must make up for what she's done wrong and show them she means that she's sorry... even if they don't know what she's done...'

Thinking time

- Do you always know when you have made a mistake?
- What should you do if you realize you have made a mistake?

Prayer

Dear God, sometimes we make mistakes and we don't mean to. Sometimes we make mistakes and we know we are making them. We're sorry when we get it wrong. Help us to put things right as often as we can. Amen

Thinking time activity

Put these mistakes in order of importance and explain your order.

a. Saying you ate four sweets when you really ate nine.

b. Saying you know nothing about it when really it was you who broke your brother's or sister's or friend's CD.

c. Getting a calculation wrong in maths.

d. Forgetting to tell someone an important message.

Setting simple goals

I have not yet reached my goal, and I am not perfect.
But Christ has taken hold of me. So I keep on running
and struggling to take hold of the prize. My friends,
I don't feel that I have already arrived. But I forget what is
behind, and I struggle for what is ahead. I run towards the
goal, so that I can win the prize of being called to heaven.

Philippians 3:12–14

It's better not to make a promise at all than to make
one and not keep it.

Ecclesiastes 5:5

KS1: 1e: How to set simple goals.

📖 **Bible link**

The Bible tells us that it is worth striving to achieve a sought-after goal and staying focused until the prize is won. Breaking a huge task into bite-sized chunks is one way of tackling the problem of how to stay focused.

Jerome's bedroom was a mess. Mum's method of demanding he tidy it all in one go did not work. Then Gran arrived and helped him tidy his room by doing a little bit each day.

Jerome's bedroom

There were only two words to describe Jerome's bedroom. One was 'A'; the other was 'MESS'.

His mum and his sister moaned at him, and now his gran was moaning too—and his gran had only arrived half an hour ago with a huge box of chocolates, a new game and a football shirt, all for him. She had come to stay for a week because his sister was having an operation in hospital and Mum needed to be free to go to visit her.

'Leave that room and that boy to me,' Jerome heard Gran say to Mum. Jerome wasn't sure if he liked the sound of that!

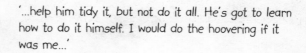

What do you think Gran is going to do?

The next morning, Gran took Jerome to school. Mum was already at the hospital with Beth.

'Tonight,' Gran said as they walked down the road, 'you and I are going to start tidying your bedroom.'

'Oh!' That sounded so boring! Jerome hoped he was going to be allowed to do something else as well.

❖

Jerome had a good day at school. The hamster escaped at lunchtime and he was the one who found it—inside the drawer where the multi-link was kept. He told Gran about it when she picked him up. Gran grinned and told him Beth's operation had gone well and that Beth was still half asleep, which was why they weren't going to visit her that evening.

'We're going to start on your bedroom instead,' Gran smiled, 'and I've made a card to help us. I'll show you when we get home.'

Jerome frowned. How on earth could a card help them tidy his room?

'MONDAY IS BOOKCASE DAY,' Jerome read out loud from the card as Gran poured him a glass of milk.

'And that's all we're going to do,' Gran said. 'Just the bookcase.'

Jerome looked at Gran. Whenever Mum tidied up his room, it took ages and ages. Just doing the bookcase didn't sound too bad.

Is it a good idea to think about big tasks as lots of smaller ones? Why?

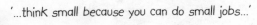

Other children have said...

'...smaller ones make it quicker...'

'...my dad told me that if you do all the big ones first it looks like you've done more...'

'...think small because you can do small jobs...'

'...you always want to complete things...'

As they were tidying the bookcase, Jerome found his favourite book about dinosaurs. He thought he had lost it or that Beth had hidden it to annoy him. He put it with his football books, which were at one end of the shelf next to his bed. On the floor was a pile of books that Jerome would never read again.

'I wonder if the children at the hospital would like to have these,' Gran said. 'Your mum could take them in tomorrow.'

Jerome thought that was a good idea.

❖

On Tuesday, after Gran and he had eaten fish fingers and chips, Gran took out another card.

'TUESDAY IS TOYBOX DAY,' Jerome read.

'Let's see what we find today,' Gran laughed as she made sure the bookcase was still tidy.

Jerome never put anything back in its box, so his plastic spacemen and his wooden train set and his mega-monsters and his soldiers were all mixed up with board games and dice and counters and bits of fluff and dead spiders and buttons and Lego and crayons and five dirty odd socks that were hard and smelly, and the insides of the doll's house and little football players and… it was a right mess.

Gran cleared a space on the carpet, heaved the box into the space and pushed it over so that everything tipped out. Then she and Jerome began sorting everything out.

'There,' Gran said at last. 'All done.'

The toys he played with most were now on the spare shelf of the bookcase. On the carpet was a pile of toys that Jerome wouldn't play with again because he had grown out of them, and in the box were things he sometimes used. The five smelly socks were in the washing basket in the bathroom. Jerome had taken them there himself.

'Shall we take these to the hospital as well?' Gran suggested, pointing at the pile of toys on the carpet. 'Your mum said we could go for evening visiting tonight.'

So they packed the toys in plastic bags and took them. The nurses were really pleased.

'So you're Beth's brother, are you?' one of them said, as Gran and Jerome went to the desk to find out where Beth and Mum were. 'Your mum was telling me about you today. Said you support Manchester United, is that right?'

Jerome nodded.

'Well, I support Arsenal,' the nurse grinned, 'but we won't fall out over it. They're down there. The bed by the window.'

Beth had a huge bandage on her leg and had to lie very still. She could talk, though, and move her arms. She and Jerome played cards while Gran and Mum went to the canteen to find something for Mum to eat.

❖

On Wednesday, Gran wanted to tidy and clean the carpet and everything that touched it. She pulled Jerome's bed out and vacuumed all the fluff and dust. It made Jerome cough. Then he had to help while she moved his table and rug and the boxes that lived under the windowsill. She even cleaned under and behind the cupboard where his clothes were kept.

'What are these?' she said, holding up a very muddy pair of football boots.

'My boots!' Jerome shouted. He had lost them ages ago. Mum had been ever so cross with him.

'And they were under your cupboard all the time,' Gran sighed. 'What are we going to do with you? Do they still fit?'

Jerome tried them on. They were too small now.

'My feet keep growing,' he said.

'It's what happens,' Gran commented. 'Put the boots at the top of the stairs, then come and help me put the rug back in its proper place.' He did as she asked. The room smelt fresher and cleaner. 'We can play on the floor now,' Gran said. 'Shall we make a town? You've got some train track and a plastic road and we could make some houses out of Lego.'

So they did. The town they made was lovely. Jerome showed it to Mum when she came home later that evening.

'That's fantastic,' she said. 'Shall we leave it up for a few days? You can show Beth when she comes out of hospital on Friday.'

'Jerome,' Gran suddenly said, staring at the bookcase, 'why is there a dirty sock on your bookcase?'

They all looked. One black sock with green stripes round the top stared back at them.

'It must have jumped up there all by itself,' Jerome said.

'And where should a dirty sock be?' Gran asked.
'In the washing basket,' Jerome replied.
'So what are you going to do now?'
Jerome stood up.
'Thank you,' Gran said and smiled at Mum.

❖

'You know what?' Gran said on Thursday as she picked Jerome up from school. 'We're going to sort through that big box of dressing-up clothes tonight.'

Gran didn't just sort the clothes out, though. Gran told stories and Jerome dressed up as she told them. The pirate with a crooked nose fell down a hole when he was searching for treasure, the policeman caught a robber by tripping him up, the pop star fell off the stage in the middle of his song. Gran was great at telling stories and, before they knew it, the box was tidy and put away again.

At school on Friday, Jerome was awarded a certificate because he had done so well with his maths. He grinned from ear to ear as his teacher told everyone in the class how hard he had worked. That wasn't the only good thing to happen, though, because Gran took him shopping when he came out of school. They left Jerome's certificate in her car.

'We might lose it if we take it with us,' she said.

'What are we going to buy?' Jerome asked.

'Well, young man,' Gran smiled, 'I think you've been so good about tidying your room, and coping with your sister being in hospital and your mum being out so much, that I want to buy you some new curtains, a new lampshade, a new noticeboard and a new pair of football boots. And I thought we could buy Beth a new CD. She's been very sensible as well.'

Today was definitely a good day!

On Saturday, Manchester United scored four goals and won their match. Jerome told Gran about it when he phoned her in the evening.

What do you think about setting goals for yourself?

Other children have said...

'...you have to give yourself something that is a challenge...'

'...I don't because I never reach my target...'

'...I always give up before I reach them...'

'...they help me, but I had to learn to set good ones... I mean, small ones I can achieve...'

What does it feel like when you achieve one of them?

Other children have said...

'...great, cheerful, on top of the world...'

'...proud, want to set more and get there...'

'...makes me want to be challenged more...'

Other things children have said

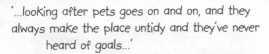

'...looking after pets goes on and on, and they always make the place untidy and they've never heard of goals...'

'...if you achieve, you should be able to tell someone, like your mum or your dad or your best friend. Even a teacher would do...'

Thinking time

- Do different people have different goals? Why?
- Think of a lesson you really like. What goal could you set yourself in that lesson?

- Think of the lesson you like least. What goal could you set for that one?
- Is setting goals a good idea? Why?
- What sort of reward would you like to give yourself for achieving your goal?

Prayer

Dear God, it's great when I manage to do something really well. I feel all good inside and everyone smiles at me and it makes me want to do even more and get better. Thank you for all the things I can do. Amen

Thinking time activity

Think of some small goals to help you do something you would like to achieve. Write four goals on separate pieces of paper and pin them to a noticeboard, or use a fridge magnet to keep them on the fridge door until you have completed the task.

Looking after
living things

Our Lord, by your wisdom you made so many things;
the whole earth is covered with your living
creatures... All of these depend on you to provide
them with food, and you feed each one with your
own hand, until they are full.

Psalm 104:24, 27–28

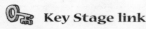

Key Stage link

KS1: 2e: To realize that people and other living things have needs, and that they have responsibilities to meet them.

Bible link

All living things need looking after and Christians believe that God has put people in charge of managing them. In this story, Jasmine and Paul look after their neighbour's cat and plants— and face up to the consequences.

Alfie, the cyclamen and Grandad

Whenever Mrs Stibbs went on holiday, Jasmine and Paul's mum looked after her plants and fed the cat.

'Alfie will need a bit of loving,' Mrs Stibbs said when she left the key at their house the day before she headed off for Spain. 'And watch out for his claws. If you're too rough with him he'll stick them in you and then you'll know all about it. And don't forget, the umbrella plant has to be covered in water all the time. It's the tall one in the porch with sticky-up leaves that looks like an umbrella.'

'Don't you worry,' Mum said. 'We've looked after them before and they've been all right. You just go and have a fantastic time with all that sun and food and sitting with your feet up.'

Other children have said...

'...light and air...'

'...food. My cat eats Whiskas and won't touch that cheap stuff my mum gets sometimes. She gets really cross with him and tries to hide it by mixing them up, but he still won't touch it...'

'...oxygen and somewhere to live...'

'...love. My mum talks to her plants when she waters them and we all laugh at her...'

Mrs Stibbs left on Saturday morning just as Jasmine and Paul were off to see Grandad, who lived on the other side of town. They waved as the taxi pulled away. Grandad had a cat called Malcolm, a canary called George, a goldfish called Winston and a tin full of chocolate biscuits, which was half empty by the time Jasmine and Paul returned home at six o'clock that evening.

Alfie was waiting for them, sitting by their front door, purring.

'I'm sure he can understand what people say,' Mum laughed. 'He knows we're looking after him. Let's go and feed him now.'

Mrs Stibbs' house key was on a keyring with a monkey dangling from it. Mum unlocked the porch door first, then the front door. Alfie meanwhile raced round the side of the house and dived through the catflap in the back door. He was sitting in the hall waiting for them and followed Mum into the kitchen, watching her carefully as she took a half-finished can of cat food out of the fridge. Then he sprang on to the work surface and tried to stick his nose in the can while Mum spooned the food out of it.

'You're a very funny little black cat,' she told him, 'with sticking-out ears and a great fat hungry stomach.' Alfie purred even louder. 'There, your food's ready now.' She lowered the plastic dish on to the mat by the kitchen door. Alfie followed it and crouched low, sticking his face into the food.

Sunday came and went, and on Monday the plants needed checking as well.

'They'll need a very little bit of water,' Mum told Jasmine as she filled up the watering-can at the sink. 'Except the umbrella plant. That will need to be covered.'

Jasmine carefully carried the can to the front room. On the windowsill was a plant—a beautiful cyclamen with deep red flowers that looked like fairies' wings. The soil was moist but not wet so Jasmine lifted the watering-can and in two seconds the soil round the cyclamen was covered with water.

'That's better,' she whispered. 'I'll look after you, little plant.' Then she headed for the porch. The umbrella plant pot needed topping up as well. In all, she found six plants downstairs and one upstairs (in the bathroom) and carefully watered them all.

By the time she had finished, Mum and Paul had fed Alfie, put the post on the kitchen table and checked all the rooms in the house. Everything was fine.

'Well done!' Mum said as she once more locked the front door and then the porch door.

❖

It was Wednesday morning when they noticed that Alfie was limping. It seemed to be his back right paw that was causing him trouble.

'Let me have a look, little one,' Mum said gently, but Alfie had no intention of letting anyone near his paw and spat and hissed at her.

'OK, then,' Mum said, backing off. 'I've got to take Jasmine and Paul to school. Then I'll come back and have another look at you.'

But, half an hour later, Alfie still wouldn't let Mum have a look at his back paw. She decided to leave him until the evening and see if he was better then.

As soon as Jasmine came out of school, she asked about Alfie.

'I've been worried about him all day,' she said. 'We've got to go and see how he is.'

As they walked past Mrs Stibbs' front window, Mum noticed the beautiful red fairy flowers of the cyclamen. They weren't standing tall any more, but drooping.

'I wonder what's happened to that plant,' she said.

'I've been watering it, Mum,' Jasmine said.

'Oh,' Mum said. 'How much water?'

'Like the umbrella plant.'

'Ah!' Mum said again. 'My fault—I should have told you. Cyclamens like a bit of water poured down the side of their pot, never ever over the top of them.'

Jasmine felt awful. She hadn't meant to kill the plant.

'Right,' Mum said, 'we'll pour all the water off and leave the pot in the sink to drain. That might save it. Now where's the cat? I'm more worried about him than I am the plant.'

Alfie was nowhere to be seen. Neither had he finished his breakfast. Half of it was still in his plastic bowl. Paul found him lying on Mrs Stibbs' bed. His eyes were half-shut and he didn't stretch and yawn and purr like he usually did.

'I think you need to go to the vet,' Mum sighed, stroking Alfie's head. 'You're not very well, are you?'

'How will we get him there?' Paul asked.

'Mrs Stibbs must have a travelling box somewhere, but I don't know where,' Mum said. 'We'll have to borrow Malcolm's travelling cat box from Grandad.'

So they locked Mrs Stibbs' house up and drove over to see Grandad, who thought it was great having an extra visit from them and wanted to know all about Alfie. Grandad gave Paul and Jasmine a chocolate biscuit each when Mum wasn't looking.

'You will phone and let me know what happens, won't you?' he said as they left.

'We will,' Mum promised.

Why is it important for older people to be in contact with other people?

Other children have said...

'...because of diseases and they get lonely...'

'...I wish my grandparents lived nearer. They live in London and we never see them. Shireen does, all the time.'

'...they might need help...'

'...it's boring for them if they are on their own...'

The vet explained that Alfie had an infection in his back paw and that was making him feel ill.

'He'll need some antibiotics,' she said. 'That should sort him out in a day or two. I'll give him his first one now.'

Mum thought about letting Alfie sleep in their kitchen that night but, in the end, decided he would be better in his own house. By the next evening Alfie was feeling much better and even purring. Paul sat next to him and stroked his long black fur.

'You're going to be all right now,' he told him, then screeched in pain. He snatched his hand away from Alfie's sharp claws.

'Ow! Mum, the cat just scratched me and I'm bleeding.'

Why do you think Alfie scratched Paul?

Other children have said...

'...he got too close to his hurt...'

'...cats like to be left alone sometimes...'

'...he doesn't like being fussed. Our cat's like that and suddenly lashes out at you. My dad got his nose scratched last weekend...'

'Maybe he just wants to be left in peace,' Mum suggested. 'We'll clean the scratch and put a plaster on it when we get home. Let me just check the cyclamen.'

'Is it going to be all right?' Jasmine asked. She was still a bit worried about it.

'I think so,' Mum said. 'We spotted it just in time. You have to remember, if it's alive it needs looking after in its own special way.'

'Am I alive?' Jasmine said, staying absolutely still. Mum looked at her doubtfully, then tickled her. Jasmine laughed.

'I think you probably are,' Mum said.

Other things children have said

'...everyone needs caring for and looking after, even if they think they're all right...'

'...everyone needs love...'

'...being alive is hard work...'

Thinking time

- Who looks after you in a special way?
- Can some plants survive without water?
- Do you help to look after anything that is alive? How?
- Think of three good things you've done to help someone or something that is alive.
  Put in order the five most important things a person needs.

Prayer

Dear God, anything that is alive is special and needs looking after if it is to grow and stay healthy. Sometimes it's easy to do that. Sometimes it's hard. Help us to keep going when it seems difficult. Thank you for our families and pets. Amen

Thinking time activity

Make a list of all the things you have at home that need looking after in a special way.

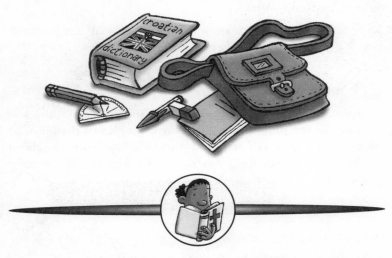

Cultural
differences

The Lord said to Abram: 'Leave your country, your
family, and your relatives and go to the land that
I will show you.'

Genesis 12:1

There are many different languages in this world, and
all of them make sense. But if I don't understand the
language that someone is using, we will be like
foreigners to each other.

1 Corinthians 14:10–11

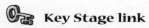

Key Stage link

KS2: 2e: To reflect on spiritual, moral, social and cultural issues... to understand other people's experiences.

Bible link

Understanding how other people live in distant countries is difficult. In the Bible there are many examples of people who moved to a new country and thrived. This story is about Robbie, who moves from America to Croatia and faces many changes.

It's so different

Croatia is a very special place. At least, that was what Robbie's mother told him. A lady in a huge coat smiled at them as they came down the steps from the aeroplane.

'Dobra dan,' she greeted everyone. 'Welcome to Zagreb.'

The air was cold. Robbie could see his breath in it.

'I think "dobra dan" means "hello",' his mother whispered. Not that Robbie was listening. He had spotted the cream and green military helicopters in a field nearby, their rotor blades dangling loosely from a central metal column.

Suddenly he wanted to be back in America, back with his friends, his house with its heated swimming-pool and streets with restaurants and fast cars zig-zagging up the highway. Only he was here, aged nine, on what he had been told was an exciting adventure—which meant he had to learn another language, meet lots of new people, leave all his friends behind and find out what life was like in a different part of the world.

Dad would still be working at a university where most people spoke American, and Mum would still be writing newspaper articles, just as she did back home. It was all right for them. He was the one going to a new school. What if the other children didn't like him because he was American? He'd seen a programme on television once about people from different countries not being liked just because of where they came from. It didn't matter what the person was like—if they came from the wrong country, everyone was horrible to them. That might happen to him.

Robbie was so tired. All he wanted was his bed—his nice comfy bed, back in America. But there was Dad, waiting for them, grinning and smiling and coming towards them with his arms out for a hug. He had been in Zagreb, the capital of Croatia, for a month already.

What has Robbie got to learn?

Other children have said...

'...the language will be the hardest because you can't see it...'

'...what's dangerous...'

'...the way people act...'

'...every country has its own traditions and he won't know any of those and will feel left out...'

'...he might insult someone and not realize it...'

'...school. That's hard even if you understand the language, and Robbie doesn't...'

'You'll love the apartment,' Dad told them as he swung their suitcases into the back of his car. 'And, Robbie, the school you're going to is just fine. I went there last week and spoke to the head teacher. You'll have English lessons, which you'll find dead easy, and they're going to give you extra lessons to help you learn to speak Croatian.' Extra lessons. Who wanted those? Robbie certainly didn't!

They were driving along a fast road now. Robbie looked at the adverts along the side of it. The letters had squiggles sticking up and hanging down from them. He was going to have to learn what they meant.

'I want to go back home,' he whispered to himself. 'Please, let me go back.'

It only took 15 minutes to reach the block of apartments where they would be living. Old cars littered the street, but there was a park at the end of it. Maybe he could play baseball there—or maybe not.

The tiny lift up to their apartment was plastered in graffiti and smelt dirty. At the second floor, the lift doors opened and Robbie just had time to see a concrete landing before the lights went out.

'Stay here and I'll put the lights back on,' Dad said and disappeared into the semi-darkness. 'We have one minute before they go off again,' he said ten seconds later. Paint was peeling off the iron railings by the stairs, and it felt cold.

'That's our door,' Dad pointed out, 'at the far end of the landing. Be quick, or the lights will go out again.' He helped them with their cases, then took out the key.

If you had a small amount of money to spend on an apartment block to make it better, what would you spend it on?

Other children have said...

'...I wouldn't bother. It'd only get smashed up again...'

'...paint and cleaning stuff...'

'...pay an electrician to make sure the lights stayed on for longer...'

'...lights...'

'...I'd paint proper graffiti...'

To Robbie's surprise, the apartment was all right. It was smaller than their house in America, but very cosy. Robbie had a computer in his bedroom and he could see the park from his window. Some children were playing football.

What is going to be the hardest thing for Robbie when he tries to make friends?

Other children have said...

'...they might not like him because he's American...'

'...the language...'

'...he won't be able to make them laugh because they won't understand him, and if they don't laugh they won't relax with him...'

Dad had a meal ready for them, but the food tasted odd and neither Robbie nor Mum were hungry. They had been travelling for 17 hours and all they really wanted to do was go to bed and sleep—which is exactly what they both did.

In the morning, Robbie and Mum woke up too early. Their bodies were still on American time.

'You'll find it strange at first,' Dad said. 'I did, but I got used to it and now it's OK.' Robbie shut his eyes and wished he were back home again.

❖

That day, he and Mum got used to their new home. They were jet-lagged and kept wanting to fall asleep. In the afternoon they visited the market in the middle of Zagreb. It was full of vegetables and fruit laid out on tables. Mum bought some and got confused with the different money she now had to use. Then they went to the cathedral behind the market. It had lots of gold paintings and stained-glass windows and pictures, and was a bit like the one back home. There was something nice about that.

> **Why do religions have signs and symbols that are the same all over the world?**

Other children have said...

'...because religions are for everyone and it doesn't matter where you are...'

'...people who believe the same thing have the same symbols, like crosses and wine...'

On Monday, Dad took Robbie to his new school. There were 25 other children in his class. The teacher smiled at him. She spoke a little English and asked Miro to look after him.

'Dobro dan,' Miro said and smiled in a friendly sort of way. That was what the lady at the airport had said to them.

'Dow—bro dan,' Robbie tried back. But everyone was laughing at him. Was it because he had tried to speak their language and got it wrong?

'Dobro,' Miro repeated slowly. 'D – o – bro.'

He made the 'o' sound short as in 'ox'.

'Dobro,' Robbie said. Miro put his thumb up and smiled again. Lots of the other children were smiling as well.

Once Robbie was settled in, the teacher carried on with the lesson—in Croatian. Robbie looked at the pictures in the books they were using. There were maps, so he decided it was a geography lesson. When everyone started writing, the teacher came to his table and tried to explain it to him, only her English wasn't that good.

What could a school do to help a child who does not speak the national language?

Other children have said...

'...give him lots of friends and let them teach him...'

'...give him extra lessons to help him, only they should be in school time...'

'...have someone sit next to him and translate what the teacher says into his own language until he understands...'

Is this a good use of the school's and country's resources when Robbie is only going to be there for three years?

Other children have said...

'...his parents should be asked to pay for it...'

'...yes, because he needs to know the language and he might come back to the country when he is older...'

By the end of his first day at school, Robbie had learned how to say three very important words—'please' (*molim*), 'thank you' (*hvala*) and 'toilet' (*toaleta*). He also liked the fact that his new school had a break at ten o'clock for a snack—he had pizza and chips—and finished lessons at lunch time, with clubs in the afternoon. He played football with Miro and some of the other boys and was as good as, if not better than, most of them.

'Well,' Mum said, when he arrived back at the apartment, 'How was it?'

Robbie screwed his nose up. It had been 'all right' but not brilliant. It could have been worse, and tomorrow he would learn some more new words.

Other things children have said

'...Mum needs to let him bring his new friends back to where they live...'

'...he should only be spoken to in Croatian, then he would have to learn...'

- Do you know anyone who has come from another country? How did they get on when they first arrived?
- What would help someone the most?
- How would you feel if you were Robbie and everything seemed to be different from what you were used to?

Prayer

Dear God, it's hard when we go to new places, especially if we can't understand what is happening. There are many people facing that today. Help those they are with to be kind and patient. Amen

Thinking time activity

Make a list of the ten things you would find the hardest if you went to live in another country. Put them in order, with the hardest things at the top of the list.

Decision making

It is truly wonderful when relatives live together in peace. It is as beautiful as olive oil poured on Aaron's head and running down his beard and the collar of his robe. It is like the dew from Mount Hermon, falling on Zion's mountains, where the Lord has promised to bless his people with life for evermore.

Psalm 133:1–3

God has also given each of us different gifts to use...
If we can serve others, we should serve. If we can teach, we should teach. If we can encourage others, we should encourage them. If we can give, we should be generous. If we are leaders, we should do our best. If we are good to others, we should do it cheerfully.

Romans 12:6a, 7–8

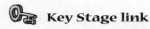

Key Stage link

KS2: 2g: To know what democracy is.

Bible link

Children find out about democracy from first-hand experience very early on in their lives. The Bible is clear that people should play to their strengths and work together. In this story, issues are raised when Josie is challenged by her older cousins, who think they know more than she does.

Stop bossing me around

Josie was four when she left England and went to live on a Greek island. In winter her father looked after his 700 olive trees. Josie liked it best when they harvested the crop in October. For that they worked in teams of four, stripping the olives off the trees before pruning them. Now she was eight, she was allowed to help with the job. Some of the trees were 2000 years old. You could tell the really old ones because they had hollow insides.

The olives were collected into barrels and sold at the end of each spring, just as Josie's father started doing his other job, which was running boat trips for tourists. He took them to the south of the island looking for turtles, and on their way back they would look at the caves where minerals from the rocks made the water appear to be a deep shade of blue. He also had a crazy golf course by the beach.

Dad liked Josie helping him with the crazy golf because she spoke both Greek and English. They made a good team. He was in charge and she was his helper. She helped collect the money and hand out putters, golf balls, score sheets and little pencils.

She also helped sweep the Astroturf if grit got on it. Their crazy golf was the best on the island, especially with the new waterfall putt Dad built last year.

Is it important to know who is in charge when you are doing something? Why?

Other children have said...

'...yes, so you can get jobs done. Someone has to tell you what to do...'

'...yes, because then you have someone to tell you the rules...'

'...yes, so you know who's going to boss you around, and if you don't like them you don't do it...'

That summer, Josie's two cousins came to stay for a week. George was thirteen and Sophie was ten. They were going to have to help as well.

'They'll probably enjoy it,' Dad said the day before they arrived.

They did. In fact, they loved it—polishing the boat in the morning and going on the crazy golf if no one was around. In the afternoons they went swimming in the sea and ate at the restaurant opposite the crazy golf course. Dad knew the owner, who gave them free pizzas if they helped tidy up. Everything was going really well until Wednesday, when the olive trees needed spraying.

'Mum's going to the orchard to do the spraying and I'm doing the boat trips, which means you three are going to be in charge of the crazy golf,' Dad said as they ate their breakfast.

'George is the oldest, so he'll be in charge. Is that all right?'

Although she nodded, Josie felt a bit hurt. She knew what to do better than George, and she spoke Greek, which he didn't. But Dad had put him in charge and that was that.

Is age important when being a leader or in charge of something?

Other children have said...

'...no, often younger people do a job better. It's practice and experience that counts...'

'...it should always be the best person...'

'...sometimes older people are better, sometimes younger. It depends on what needs to be done...'

Poor Josie. Before long, George, and then Sophie, began bossing her around.

'You sweep the course,' Sophie told her, sitting on the chair behind the kiosk.

'And when you've finished that, the water on the fountain hole needs topping up,' George added. He had put himself in charge of the money and elbowed Josie out of the kiosk when she tried to get in earlier.

'Hey, stop bossing me around,' Josie shouted, pouting her lips. Tears were pricking at the back of her eyes. She could have managed quite well without either of her cousins being there.

Is being bossy a good thing when you are working in a team?

At lunch time, Dad came to check they were all right. His next boat trip was not until half past two.

'Everything OK?' he asked.

'Great,' George piped up. 'It's brill doing this.'

'Can one of you take your food wrappers to the bin, please, to keep the place neat and tidy?' he asked.

'I will,' Josie said. She didn't mind doing things for her dad.

'...because she knew her dad was really the boss...'

'...because she trusted him and loved him too...'

'...he asked her nicely and didn't boss her around like the others did...'

Dad came with her.

'You OK?' he asked. 'You look really fed up.'

'I hate them,' she exploded. 'They boss me around all the time and ignore me if I say anything.'

Dad was a bit taken aback. 'I thought you got on all right with them.'

'It was all right until today. Today they think they're in charge, and I hate them.'

'Right,' Dad said when they returned to the kiosk and two more customers had been served. 'Here's what can happen this afternoon. Mum's still spraying the trees, but I have three spaces left in my boat. If you want, we can close the crazy golf down for a couple of hours and you can all come for a boat ride, but you'll all have to agree. I can't leave one of you here on your own. Josie, you're too young to be left on your own, and George and Sophie, you two don't speak Greek, so if there was a problem you couldn't cope.'

'I vote we go on the boat,' George said straight away, loudly.

'And me,' Sophie joined in.

'And Josie?' Dad asked.

'I want to stay here.'

Dad sighed. 'Looks like it's the boat trip,' he said. He ruffled Josie's hair. 'I want the best for all of you, so I think you'll have to come with me.'

Josie looked at the ground.

'Tell you what,' Dad said. 'Do you want to sit in the driver's seat with me?'

Maybe Josie's afternoon wouldn't be so bad after all.

Other things children have said

'...Dad didn't spoil Josie. If he had, he would have let her stay, and that wasn't what the other two wanted...'

'...you want to get as many people to enjoy themselves as possible, but you have to think about what will happen tomorrow as well and if that is the right thing to do...'

'...being responsible is very important, especially if you're in charge of something...'

Thinking time

- Which decisions do governments have to make? Are they always democratic?
- Which decisions are made at school or at home or at a club you go to? Do you always agree with those decisions?
- Is this the same in every country in the world?
- Can you say what the word 'democracy' means?

Prayer

Dear God, thank you that you have given us brains that can think and make decisions. Help us to try to do what is best for most people. More importantly, help us to be honest and treat others as we would want to be treated ourselves. Amen

Thinking time activity

How can you best let someone know you don't agree with something they have said? In pairs, role-play your ideas.

Telling the truth in the news

Everyone was excited and confused. Some of them even kept asking each other, 'What does all this mean?' Others made fun of the Lord's followers and said, 'They are drunk.'

Acts 2:12–13

Do not tell lies about others.

Exodus 20:16

KS2: 2k: To explore how the media present information.

📖 **Bible link**

The media play an important role in our society, informing and shaping opinions. The Bible recounts instances when incorrect information was given about events. Children must be taught to question the truth of news reports. In this story, when Azad was doing his paper round he came across a burglary. The press reported it—incorrectly.

Ali's forty thieves

Azad loved doing his newspaper round. He loved it for two reasons. One, he got paid. Two, Keith Swingot's house was on his round. That was something special, because Keith Swingot played football—and we're not talking first or second division here, we're talking Premiership.

Every morning, Azad would walk up the long sweeping drive towards Keith's house, hoping to see the footballer going for an early morning jog with his three labradors and personal trainer—or even glimpse the beautiful Lucy Swingot, Keith's wife, who was a model. Only he never did, because Keith Swingot had another house which was even bigger and better. The newspapers Azad delivered were for Mr Jones the caretaker, who looked after the house when Keith wasn't living there.

Other children have said...

'...from newspapers. That's where you get to know what famous people are doing...'

'...people always want to know about famous people...'

'...someone knew him and told him...'

It was a Friday when it happened, just after seven o'clock as Azad walked up Keith Swingot's drive. He heard what sounded like glass being broken, coming from the back of the house.

Now Azad's dad was a policeman and always said that if Azad came across anything unusual, that might be dangerous, he was not to get involved or try to be a hero. So Azad stopped where he was and coughed, very loudly, just to let whoever it was know that someone else was there. Then he rushed as fast as he could back down the drive and waved frantically at the first car that came along. The driver pulled over.

'What's up?' asked a young man in a smart suit, leaning over the passenger seat.

'That's Keith Swingot's house,' Azad panted.

'What? *The* Keith Swingot?'

Azad nodded.

'Someone's just broken a window... at the back of the house... my dad says I should call the police.'

'Who's your dad, then? Is he famous as well?'

'No, he's a policeman.'

'Oh. If he's a policeman, we'd better do it, then. Are you sure it was glass you heard?'

'Well, I think so… it was round the back of the house and I was at the front…'

The young man pulled out his mobile phone and dialled 999. Within a minute, the police knew what Azad had heard and were on their way. Three minutes and 22 seconds later, a police car zoomed round the corner. Azad was standing by the gates as the car drove up the drive. He then watched as two policemen went round to the back of the house.

'You're a smart one,' they said to Azad when they reappeared a few minutes later. 'Looks like they broke the glass and then ran. Left a trowel behind. Hopefully, there'll be some finger-prints on that. Well done, young man.'

Azad smiled. He told the police exactly what he had heard and seen, which wasn't much but was better than nothing.

What details would Azad have been able to give to the policeman?

Other children have said…

'…the noise he heard. The fact that he coughed to show the people he was there. His name and address…'

'…he thought they might be thieves…'

'…that it was the man in the car who called the police…'

'And is Keith Swingot inside the house?' Azad asked, hopefully, as they finished. The policeman shook his head.

'We woke the caretaker up. He was asleep on the other side of the house when it happened and didn't hear anything.' The policeman wrote down Azad's name and address, thanked him again and said he could carry on with his paper round.

❖

It was about ten minutes later when a woman dressed in jeans and a polo-neck jumper walked towards them. She had a notebook in her hand and a camera bag slung over her shoulder.

'Moira Johnston, reporter,' she introduced herself and tried to shake Azad's hand. 'Hear there's been a break-in at the Swingots' house. Is that right? Are you the paper boy who found the thieves?'

Azad stopped walking and nodded.

'You dialled 999 at five past seven and it's ten to eight now,' she carried on. 'Were the police slow in answering your call?'

'No,' he said, glancing at his watch to check the time. He was running late and would get into trouble if he were late for school. So he answered either 'yes', 'no' or 'I can't remember' to all the questions Moira Johnston asked him, and after a couple of minutes she left him alone.

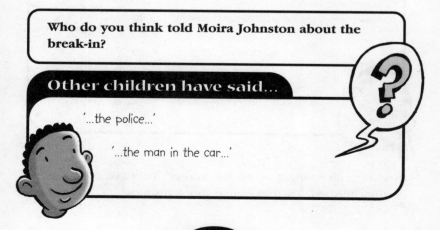

Who do you think told Moira Johnston about the break-in?

Other children have said...

'...the police...'

'...the man in the car...'

Azad went as fast as he could and was only fifteen minutes late when he got home. He told his Mum what had happened.

'Well done,' she said when he finished. 'I'm proud of you. Dad will be as well. You're so sensible.'

Mum and Dad weren't the only ones who were proud. The local newspaper was as well. 'ALI'S FORTY THIEVES' the headline read the following evening.

Azad Ali, 10, stopped thieves in their tracks at footballer Keith Swingot's house yesterday. The brave newspaper boy disturbed their night's thieving when he heard glass being shattered. He raced to the road and flagged down a passing car, driven by George Holmes, 22, of Stockton Lane. Mr Holmes, manager of Passports Suitcase Superstore, said it could have been very dangerous but Azad was not worried about his own safety and simply wanted the thieves caught and punished. Azad borrowed Mr Holmes's mobile phone to call the police station and then waited for over 20 minutes for them to arrive—the long delay in spite of police promises to arrive at crime scenes as quickly as possible.

After giving a description of the thieves to the police, Azad continued his newspaper round before going to school. Azad knew what to do because his father, Constable Ali, 54, works for the local police force and has told his son exactly what to do. Mr Swingot was delighted that the thieves had been stopped and is going to contact brave Azad to offer him a reward.

'You're 44,' Mum howled with laughter, 'not 54.'

'Huh!' Dad said. 'And has Keith Swingot offered you a reward? Because if he has, you haven't told us about it.'

'I haven't heard a thing,' Azad said. But maybe Keith Swingot would feel he had to give him one now.

'How did that reporter know you were a policeman, Dad? I never told her,' he said.

His father looked at him. 'Did you tell George Holmes, 22, of

Stockton Lane, manager of Passports Suitcase Superstore, that I was one?'

Azad frowned. 'Yes, I did,' he said slowly.

Dad sighed. 'The press find out all sorts of things about all sorts of people. Sometimes it's a good thing and stops people doing things they shouldn't do. Sometimes it's a bad thing.'

What details has the newspaper article got wrong?

Other children have said...

'...it said the police took 20 minutes, and Azad never saw the thieves so he couldn't give a description...'

'...that Azad wanted to get the thieves punished...'

'...how old his dad was...'

'...the reward...'

Other things children have said

'...newspapers are right some of the time...'

'...everyone reads newspapers. They have pictures sometimes as well...'

'...you shouldn't tell lies, not even in newspapers...'

'...newspapers don't tell all the truth because they want to make people believe something...'

Thinking time

- How important is it to always tell the truth?
- Why do the media sometimes give their audience information that is later shown to be incorrect?
- Why do people contact newspapers with stories about other people?
- Would you tell a reporter about your best friend if your best friend had done something the press might be interested in? Why or why not?

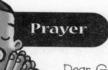

Prayer

Dear God, help me always to tell the truth and never be disloyal to people who trust me. Amen

Thinking time activity

Write your own, accurate, article about what Azad actually did. Then write one that doesn't quite tell the truth.

Resisting peer pressure

If you do the right thing, honesty will be your guide. But if you are crooked, you will be trapped by your own dishonesty.

Proverbs 11:3

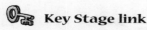 **Key Stage link**

 Bible link

Learning to say 'no' is important and is part of discovering how to stand up for what is right. Christians believe that standing up for what is right is an essential part of an honest relationship. But it is very difficult when it is friends or family who are applying pressure to behave in a risky way. Mitch, who was no angel, saw a different side to his sister one evening when she was left in charge of him. It was a side he was not too happy with.

Back off!

Mitch (or Mitchell, as he was called by his grandmother) and Marnie (or Mark, as he was called by his grandfather) were identical twins. Their feet, their hair, their elbows, their skin were completely the same. They even had the same pattern of freckles on their knees. But inside they were as different as a staple gun is from a dustbin.

According to most adults, Marnie was perfect. He worked hard at school, tidied his side of the bedroom, never said anything rude and smiled at everyone he met.

'What a lovely boy your Marnie is,' people would say to Mrs Greenway. And she would smile and think how lucky she was to have him and what a brilliant mother she must be.

She needed to think that sometimes, because Mitch was exactly the opposite. He would 'break wind', as his mother called it (he and his friends called it something else), whenever

he was bored, and belch in the middle of lessons. That was when he wasn't whistling quietly to himself. Worst of all, he picked his nose and flicked whatever he found inside at people he didn't like. He was also fed up with being told he should behave like his brother.

'Why can't you be like Marnie?' people would say to him.

Because I don't want to be, he would think to himself. I want to be me. I do not want to be like my brother. I never have done and never will. So back off.

Now Marnie and Mitch had an older sister called Jen (or Jennifer, as Mr Greenway called her when he was telling her off). She was 15 but got on all right with her twin brothers even though she was six years older than they were. Mum and Dad sometimes left Jen to babysit because she was so sensible, and they knew she would prevent Mitch from setting the house on fire or phoning Australia or shaving the cat or anything else stupid like that.

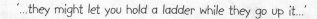

How do you know when your parents trust you?

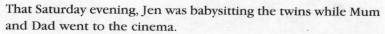

Other children have said...

'...they let you do more things and tell you more interesting things about what is going on...'

'...they might let you hold a ladder while they go up it...'

'...they ask you to do something because they know you will do it properly...'

That Saturday evening, Jen was babysitting the twins while Mum and Dad went to the cinema.

'We'll be back about eleven,' Mum said as she and Dad put on their coats, 'and I'll phone you as soon as the film has finished to make sure everything's all right.'

'OK,' Jen called out from the living-room, thinking of the ten pounds she was going to be paid. The boys had a video to watch, some food to eat and then they were going to bed, and she had no intention of even thinking about them.

❖

'Right, they've gone,' Jen shouted as the car pulled away. 'Let's get the party started!' Mitch's ears pricked up. Suddenly the television programme he and Marnie were watching became very boring.

'They've gone,' his sister was saying into her mobile phone. 'Bring some drink round with you as well. Can you make sure everyone knows they'll have to smoke outside. Don't want Mum and Dad finding out.'

'You're not supposed to have any friends round when you're babysitting,' Marnie said indignantly.

'Shut up,' Jen said.

Marnie retreated back to the settee. Mitch watched with interest. This evening could be entertaining.

❖

Five of Jen's friends turned up, all with cans and bottles of drink. Mitch knew all of them except one. He was taller than the others and had a scar running down his left cheek. He seemed to be older as well, and spoke gruffly. Mitch helped him lay the supplies of drink out on the kitchen table. It seemed a friendly sort of thing to do.

'Here, have some of this,' the boy offered Mitch, pouring something from a bottle into a mug.

'What is it?' Mitch asked.

The boy shrugged his shoulders. 'You too chicken to try?' he sneered.

'No!' Mitch said.

'Go on, then,' the boy said again.

Mitch looked at the foaming head inside the mug. It was probably beer like Dad drank.

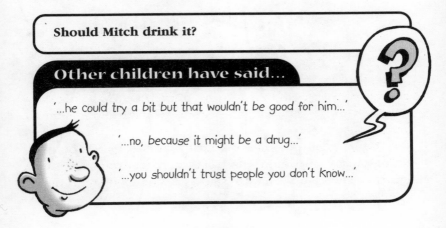

Should Mitch drink it?

Other children have said...

'...he could try a bit but that wouldn't be good for him...'

'...no, because it might be a drug...'

'...you shouldn't trust people you don't know...'

'Oi, Jase, he's only nine.' Jen's voice was behind Mitch now. 'I'm meant to be looking after him as well. That's not for you, Mitch.'

'Oh yes it is,' Jase laughed. 'Here, Titch, show me how grown up you are and drink it. All of it, mind. You're not just going to take a sip then run away.'

'Upstairs, you,' Jen ordered, snatching the mug from Mitch's hand. 'This is my party, not yours.'

'I want my supper,' Mitch argued back.

'You can come down for it later,' Jen said, flicking her long fair hair over her shoulders. She looked a bit flustered and there was a nasty edge to her voice. Three of her friends were in the kitchen now as well, with cigarettes in their mouths. She turned and unlocked the back door.

'Up,' Jen said again to Mitch.

'No,' Mitch answered back. He wanted to see if his sister was going to smoke as well.

'If you stay down, you've got to smoke one of these,' Jen said. 'Then you'll be in big trouble with Mum and Dad, because I'll tell them you smoked.'

'And I'll tell them about your friends,' Mitch answered back.

The older boy, the one Jen had called Jase, suddenly put his hands under Mitch's armpits, dragged him outside and held him against the outside wall of the house.

'Going to have your first cigarette, then, are you?' There was something dangerous about the way he spat the words out. 'Or are you going to tell Mummy and Daddy about your big sister having a few friends round while looking after the babies?'

A red light was glowing by Jen's face as she sucked in. All her friends were out there too, smoking, watching, laughing at him. Mitch could smell the smoke, disappearing up his nose like a bogey man with nowhere to go but inside him.

'Let me go!' Mitch suddenly shouted and began wriggling and punching the air with his fists. Jase laughed again and let him go.

'I'm telling Mum of you!' Mitch shouted at Jen.

'If you tell your mother anything, I'm going to beat the living daylights out of you,' Jase snarled, his fingers grabbing Mitch's shoulders as he reached the back door. 'Jen told you to get up to bed and you didn't, so...'

'Leave him, Jase,' Jen said. 'He's only teasing you, Mitch.'

She stuffed a ten-pound note into Mitch's hand. 'Get upstairs and keep this and don't say a word. Got it?'

What should you do if someone offers you money to keep quiet?

Other children have said...

'...take it and run!...'

'...ignore them...'

'...my brother did that once, only I told Mum and he got it in the neck...'

'...it depends on why they're giving you the money and what they've done...'

Mitch knew where that money had come from—Mum's purse. He had seen Jen open the drawer where Mum kept her handbag earlier that evening. He ducked down, out of Jase's grasp, and threw himself through the back door.

'He won't tell Mum or Dad.' That was Jen's voice mocking him. 'We'll be all right.'

Mitch was upstairs in ten seconds—one second for every pound he had just been given. Marnie looked up from the book he was reading.

'What's going on?' he asked.

'Nothing much,' Mitch said, trying to breathe normally.

'Glad I came upstairs, then,' Marnie sighed.

Mitch put the television on and started the video. He wasn't watching it, though. He didn't want to be a 'perfect' like Marnie, but at that moment he didn't trust Jen either. He had seen a different side to her tonight and, even though he was only nine and did lots of things himself that were naughty, he didn't want to do what she was doing.

How do you decide if something is 'right' or 'wrong'?

Other children have said...

'...you have to think what will happen next...'

'...think what you have been told by your parents...'

'...you have to think about it and make a sensible decision...'

'...ask someone what they think, but make sure they are trustworthy and see if they think the same as you...'

'...it's very hard sometimes. Sometimes it's easy and you just know...'

Mitch didn't have any supper. He didn't dare go downstairs again. When the video had finished, he crept into bed and lay there wide awake. He heard Jen's friends leave and, a few minutes later, Mum and Dad's car come back.

At breakfast the next morning, Mum commented that ten pounds had disappeared from her handbag. She asked if anyone knew anything about it.

What would you have done if you were Mitch?

Other children have said...

'...told his mum, but not when his sister was around or she might have hit him...'

'...given the ten-pound note back to his mum...'

'...I would have kept quiet but put the money back when she wasn't looking...'

Other things children have said

'...it's hard...'

'...you've got to be strong to do what you really think is right...'

Thinking time

- Have you ever been asked to do something you thought wasn't safe? What did you do?
- What should you do if you are not happy about something that is happening around you?
- Where is the safest place you know?

- Who is the safest person you know?
- Who might put pressure on you to do something unsafe?

Prayer

Dear God, it's ever so hard sometimes to say 'no' when everyone else is doing something and I want to join in because I want to be the same as them, even though I know it's not right. Help me be strong and brave. Amen

Thinking time activity

Act out scenes where you have to say 'no' to something.

Draw round your hand. On each of the fingers write the name of someone you can trust.

Knowing the difference between teasing and bullying

Be friendly with everyone. Don't be proud and feel
that you are cleverer than others... do your best to
live at peace with everyone... Don't let evil defeat you,
but defeat evil with good.

Romans 12:16, 18 and 21

⚷ Key Stage link

KS1: 4e: That there are different types of teasing and bullying.

📖 Bible link

Teasing can be funny and no one is upset. The Bible teaches very clearly that all relationships should be honest and loving. This can include teasing if everyone involved is happy with it. However, there is a fine line between teasing and bullying. Whale had enjoyed being teased for years until a new mermaid came to live nearby.

Whale goes missing

Once, long ago, in the water between the Mystical Island and the Island Beyond, the fishes and mermaids were called to a meeting beside the deserted castle. Something had happened, something that worried them all. Whale had disappeared.

'He'll be somewhere,' the chief mermaid said.

'But where?' whispered the mermaid with bunches in her hair.

'We'll find him,' added the mermaid with the silver wig. 'He's different from any other whale I know.'

❖

He was different, all right. For a start, he had a deep scar running down one of his flippers, and he wore glasses because he was short-sighted. Then there was his voice, which was all squeaky, and his eating habits, which were revolting. Would you believe, his favourite meal was sprouts and apricot jam on toast?

'I think we ought to look for him,' the Golden Cod said. 'He's been gone for over a week now.' And suddenly they all realized that they were missing him. Whale was always friendly, and laughed with them and listened to them and helped them, and they teased him because he was so special to them.

'Hello,' the mermaids would say in a squeaky voice just like his, 'and how are you today?'

'Having a whale of a time,' he would reply and give them a ride on his back.

The fish called him O-scar because of his damaged flipper. He didn't mind that because he knew they were only teasing him.

'O-scar, what funny flippers you have,' they would say.

'All the better to flip you with,' he would laugh and flip them through the water. It was like having their own theme park ride in the depths of the sea, and Whale was happy because he knew he was loved and that everyone cared about him.

Give examples of when you tease someone.

Other children have said...

'...if you call someone "ugly" in a nice voice and grin at them and they know they aren't really...'

'...if your best mate comes round and he's got a new football scarf and you say "that's horrible" but he knows you well enough to ignore you...'

'...when people have spots...'

'...when you offer someone food, then take it away as they go to get it. My dad does that, then he laughs and gives it to me...'

But Whale had gone. No one thought anything of it at first. He sometimes went off to see his friends on the other side of the islands. It was strange for him not to have told anyone, though.

The newest mermaid combed her hair. She had joined them two weeks ago. Whale had helped her find somewhere to put the seven suitcases and three big boxes she had with her when she first arrived.

'You're very quiet,' the mermaid with the silver wig suddenly said to her.

The newest mermaid carried on combing her hair.

'I said, you're very quiet,' the mermaid with the silver wig tried again.

'I think I upset him,' the newest mermaid said, looking at the sand beneath her tail.

Everyone turned to look at her. No one upset Whale—ever.

'What did you say?' asked the mermaid with the bunches in her hair.

'I told him his scar made him look stupid.'

'You what?'

'Well it does, doesn't it? It makes him look all funny. And he was annoying me because I wanted some apricot jam and thought he might take it all. You know how much he eats.'

'There are always pots of jam in the food cupboard,' the chief mermaid breathed, and the anger on her face shimmered through the water. 'That scar will never be stupid,' she added under her breath. 'Do you know how he got it?'

The newest mermaid shook her head.

'Three of us got trapped in the fishermen's nets and he rescued us. That's how he hurt himself. He got caught himself, helping us.'

There was silence. The mermaids and the fish looked at each other, then looked at the newest mermaid.

'You have said something to make Whale feel small,' the chief mermaid said. 'You have hurt him and you did it deliberately. You are a bully.'

The other mermaids gasped. Being called a bully, especially

by the chief mermaid, was very serious. They all knew that bullies were sad inside—so sad that they had to be nasty to others to try to make themselves feel better.

'What are we going to do about Whale?' Golden Cod asked. They would deal with the newest mermaid later on. Whale was far more important than this bully who had come to live with them.

'We're going to search for him,' the chief mermaid said. 'And when we find him, we'll tell him how incredibly special he is.'

And that is what they did. They swam behind the great mountain where the sprout and carrot fields were, beneath the great rocks where treasure lay in wooden cases, and inside the jagged caves where the shipwreck was. The Golden Cod even went to the far side of the furthest island, but Whale was nowhere to be found.

It was the smallest fish, Small Fry, who found him, lying by one of the goals on the football pitch, his eyes closed and his tail quivering. He was crying.

'Please come back,' Small Fry whispered. 'We need you. That newest mermaid told us what she said to you. She's a bully and there is no way she will be allowed to say anything like that to you again. Please come back.'

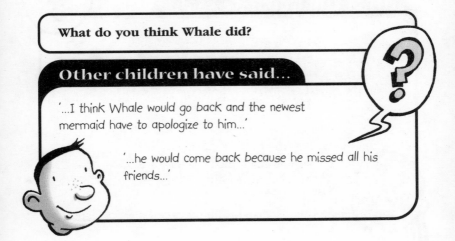

What do you think Whale did?

Other children have said...

'...I think Whale would go back and the newest mermaid have to apologize to him...'

'...he would come back because he missed all his friends...'

What do you think happened to the newest mermaid?

'...I think she left because she didn't have any friends...'

'... I think she said sorry to Whale and everyone was friends again. The newest mermaid didn't know what she was doing. She should have a second chance and prove she isn't nasty...'

'...maybe she got punished by the other mermaids...'

'...I don't know why, but I think she became Whale's closest friend...'

What are the differences between teasing and bullying?

Other children have said...

'...teasing isn't nasty and it's fun, but bullying hurts people...'

'...bullying is calling people names in a sarcastic voice...'

'...you should tell someone if you are being bullied. I told my teacher and my mum when I was bullied in year 2...'

'...bullying is mean and I don't like people who do it...'

'...bullying hurts on the inside...'

Other things children have said

'...some bullies aren't bullies all the time, just for a bit...'

'...bullies are sad inside. I stick with my friends and then no one bullies me...'

Thinking time

- What could they do to stop the newest mermaid bullying Whale?
- What would you have said to the newest mermaid?
- What would you have said to Whale?
- When does teasing become bullying?
- When have you been teased? Did you like being teased?

Prayer

Dear God, sometimes it hurts when people say things about me. Sometimes they want to hurt me, sometimes it's by accident. Help me to know what to do and help me never to hurt anyone else. Amen

Thinking time activity

Use puppets to act out a situation where teasing becomes bullying.

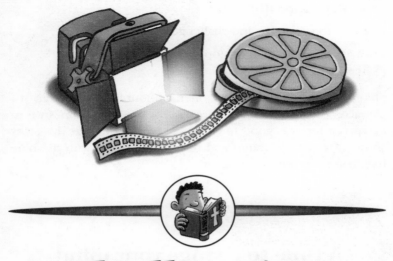

Challenging stereotypes

Live in harmony by showing love for each other.
Be united in what you think, as if you were only one
person. Don't be jealous or proud, but be humble
and consider others more important than yourselves.
Care about them as much as you care about yourselves.

Philippians 2:2–4

Key Stage link

KS2: 4e: To recognize and challenge stereotypes.

 Bible link

Stereotypes are easily formed, often without full knowledge of a character or situation. If, as Christians believe, total honesty is to be striven for, it is good to challenge typecasting—as this story shows. Are the old tramp and the bossy woman with the blue handbag really what they seem?

A time to change your mind

The old tramp's head hit the floor as he fell. Super Sofa Warehouse did not normally have people collapsing in their store.

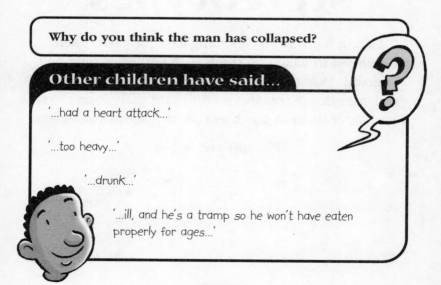

Why do you think the man has collapsed?

Other children have said...

'...had a heart attack...'

'...too heavy...'

'...drunk...'

'...ill, and he's a tramp so he won't have eaten properly for ages...'

As he fell, Sharon the shop assistant raced forward.

'Ohh!' she cried, pushing her hair behind her ears so she could see the man better.

'He's fainted, hasn't he?' one of the other shoppers said, pushing forward to have a better look.

'We'd better do something about him, hadn't we?' Sharon said slowly. Then she pulled a face. She was going to have to touch him.

At that point, a lady carrying a large blue handbag bustled forward and knelt beside the man.

'Oh!' she said in a posh voice. 'All he needs is a good slap across the cheeks. Wake up, old man! You're not on the streets now! You're in a shop. Wake up!'

And with that she slapped him twice across the cheek. Other shoppers, who had gathered round to have a look, glanced at each other, then back at the lady.

'Wake up! You've just had too much to drink. Can someone fetch a glass of water? That's all he needs.'

'I'll go,' Sharon whispered. She wasn't very good with people who were ill, and there was something about that large blue handbag and the way its owner spoke that made her a bit nervous. 'Shall I call an ambulance as well?' she mumbled. 'He could be really ill.'

'He is a tramp. Why are you suggesting we call an ambulance for him? He doesn't deserve one!' The woman's voice was shrill as she slapped the man again.

There was a gasp from the other shoppers, but none of them offered to help and stood watching until Sharon tottered back on her high heels, carrying a glass of water. The old man's head lolled from side to side as the woman with the blue handbag lifted his shoulders and tried to make him sit up before trying to pour water into his mouth. The tramp coughed and spluttered, then rolled back on to the floor again.

'Shouldn't you stick his legs in the air?' someone said. 'You could drag him over there and stick them up on one of the sofas.' There was a murmur of agreement from those watching

and several hands began dragging him towards an orange leather sofa.

'I a nurse... You wrong... Check he breathe... Look at chest... Go up and down? Check pulse but leave him on floor... No water.'

The young woman spoke with a foreign accent. The woman with the blue handbag glanced over her shoulder and scowled.

'We know what we're doing, thank you very much,' she said. 'And I wouldn't listen to you anyway,' she added. 'You should go back to where you came from.'

If the lady with the blue handbag came into the room now, what would you want to say to her?

Other children have said...

'...tell her she was pompous and bossy and should listen to other people...'

'...mean, selfish and opinionated. I don't like her...'

'...tell her to get a life...'

'...stop being so moody and take people as they are. Everyone's a person and equal to everyone else...'

The young woman didn't say anything further, but stood watching the tramp, who now had his feet up on the sofa. The woman with the blue handbag was trying to pour some more water down his throat.

Someone else stepped forward. 'I went on a first aid course, and they told us to put someone who has fainted in the recovery position and open the airways so they can breathe properly,' she said. 'Why don't you listen to this young woman? She is a nurse.'

Everyone froze and looked at the young woman as she moved to the front so that the camera could focus on her face.

'If someone collapses, never give them water or try to sit them up unless you suspect they are having a heart attack. You should assess the situation, and then carry out the ABC of first aid—check the airways are clear, check the breathing and check for circulation by feeling a pulse,' she said, without a trace of a foreign accent.

❖

'And cut! Well done, everyone. That part of the film is fine now. After lunch, we'll show what's the right thing to do when someone collapses.'

The woman with the blue handbag began helping the old man off the floor, laughing as she did so.

'You all right, Sid?' She still had a posh voice, but now it was

friendly and warm, not cruel and bossy as it had been a minute ago. 'I didn't slap you too hard, did I?'

'No,' the tramp grinned back. 'Come on, let's go and see what they've got for lunch today. You coming, Emma?'

Did your opinion of the lady with the blue handbag change when you learnt she was acting in a first aid film?

Other children have said...

'...I'm glad she knows what to do in real life...'

'...she's probably quite nice when she's not being an actor...'

Other things children have said

'...it's very important to think before you speak...'

'...the film they're making is really offensive to all sorts of people...'

'...I felt sorry for the nurse. That blue handbag lady was horrible to her...'

'...don't judge a book by its cover...'

'...you need to know all the facts before you judge someone...'

Thinking time

- What judgments do you make about what other people look like... Speak like... Dress like...?
- Do you always make sure you know all the true facts before you make a judgment about someone or something?
- How do you think people see you? Do you ever wish the way they see you was different?
- Do you actually know what famous people are like?
- What does the word 'stereotype' mean?

Prayer

Dear God, it's easy to believe what people tell us even if it's not the truth. Help us to find out the truth before we make a judgment. Amen

Thinking time activity

Invent a character that would upset everyone he or she met. How many different stereotypes can you include?

Learning to behave responsibly

I may walk through valleys as dark as death,
but I won't be afraid.

Psalm 23:4

Children, you belong to the Lord, and you do the
right thing when you obey your parents. The first
commandment with a promise says, 'Obey your father and
your mother, and you will have a long and happy life.'

Ephesians 6:1–3

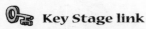

Key Stage link

KS2: 3e: To recognize the different risks in different situations. 4c: To be effective in relationships—in this case, dealing with a tragic death.

Bible link

The Bible speaks clearly about behaving responsibly and safely so that, even in difficult circumstances, we will feel safe because our trust is in God. Responsible behaviour demands looking ahead and thinking about what could happen.

Rachel and Joanna had been told what the risks were, but still decided to jump off the end of the jetty into the sea—with disastrous consequences when Rachel drowns.

The jetty

One of the first things Mum told them when they arrived at the hotel was not to jump into the sea from the end of the jetty.

'The water is very deep and there are strong currents,' she said, 'and we don't want either of you being swept out to sea, do we?'

Joanna looked enviously at the older boys who were screaming and laughing as they hurtled along the jetty before throwing themselves off the end and into the sea. There were weathered stone steps cut into the concrete wall to help them get out of the water before they ran down the jetty again. It looked such fun and she and Rachel were both good enough swimmers, even if Mum thought they weren't.

That night the two girls made up their minds.

'Your mum and dad don't have to know,' Rachel said. 'We'll sneak out of the apartment at night when they're in the bar and do it. Just once, that'll be enough.'

'But you're not supposed to go swimming in the sea when it's dark. There's a sign downstairs.'

'So? If we're not supposed to be jumping off the jetty or swimming in the dark. it'll be a double dare, double danger, double excitement and double everything! And let's do it on the last night. Your parents can't punish us then if they do find out.'

'Done!'

❖

They had a brilliant holiday. The sun was hot, the ice-creams were cold, the trips to the volcano and the old castle were great, and on Friday evening there was a concert in the hotel bar.

'We'd rather stay in our apartment on our own,' Joanna told her mum.

'Are you sure?' Her mother looked surprised. The girls had moaned about going to bed before midnight every other night.

'We're dead tired. And we've got to get up early for the plane.'

Mum frowned. She sensed they were up to something.

'I can trust you, can't I?' she said.

'Of course you can.'

Of course she could. They had been so sensible during the week.

❖

Mum and Dad only saw the first half of the concert. A shivering, sobbing Joanna appeared during the interval and the police patrol boat found Rachel's body half an hour later.

'Why did you do it?' Mum asked for the umpteenth time. They were back in their apartment now. The concert had been abandoned and Rachel's parents were being contacted in England.

'Why?' her mother asked again. But Joanna couldn't say. She wanted to hide, to pretend it hadn't happened, to go to sleep and wake up and find it was all a bad dream.

'Why couldn't it have been you that drowned?'

'Sandra!' Joanna's father gasped. 'How could you say that?'

Then Mum had her arms round Joanna, hugging her, crying again.

'I didn't mean that,' she sobbed.

'People say things they don't mean when they're upset,' her father said. He was angry and upset and guilty and nervous all at the same time.

What other things do people say that they wish they hadn't afterwards?

Other children have said...

'...that they wish they had never been born...'

'...hurtful things they don't mean...'

'...I didn't mean to do that...'

'...they might swear when they don't usually...'

Joanna still said nothing. Rachel had bought her a present, a bag covered with sequins. It was on her bed, so she couldn't have drowned. She'd walk through the door in a moment and they could all go to sleep. Only she didn't. She really had gone, really had drowned. The two of them had taken a risk and it had gone wrong.

Things were happening round Joanna and she was watching without taking part. A policewoman was saying she would be back tomorrow to interview them all again. Her father was crying while he was talking on the phone. Other

people came into the room, then went back out again. The manager of the hotel was scratching his head and talking to a policeman in Spanish. A doctor was telling her to swallow some medicine.

'It'll help you sleep,' she was told.

If only she and Rachel had gone to the concert, none of this would have happened. And what would everyone say at school? They'd all know about it. The newspaper reporters had already been to the hotel reception asking to speak to her. They were English reporters. Mum had said so.

She was a good girl, really. It had just been tonight when she hadn't been. They had wanted to be like the older boys who had been jumping off the jetty—just wanted some fun.

But Rachel hadn't been able to grasp the weathered steps, and her hands had waved frantically as the current had dragged her further and further away into the darkness, and Joanna had stood there and shouted helplessly at her friend as she disappeared.

How will Rachel's death affect Joanna?

Other children have said...

'...it'll be hard at school. Rachel's other friends might be horrible to her...'

'...she should give Rachel's mother a card and some flowers...'

'...she'll feel ill and cry a lot. Joanna has lost her best friend...'

'...she might get depressed and blame herself...'

'...nothing will make it better for her. She has to live with what happened...'

Other things children have said

'...it's OK to cry when someone dies. My dad cried at my granny's funeral...'

'...you have to think of what might happen every time you do something...'

Thinking time

- What is the hardest thing about being responsible?
- Think of all the things you do. Which have risks and which don't? What do you do about keeping yourself safe when you do something?
- What would happen if you never took any risks at all?

Prayer

Dear God, be with those who are having to deal with the consequences of their actions today. Amen

Thinking time activity

Think of five things you enjoy doing. Which has the most risk? Put them in order, with the one carrying the most risk at the top. How do you make sure you are safe? Write down some rules to keep yourself safe.

Stranger danger

No one who loves others will harm them.

Romans 13:10

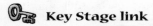 **Key Stage link**

KS1: 3e: To recognize the different risks in different situations and then decide how to behave responsibly.

 Bible link

Sadly, not everyone follows the Bible's portrayal of love that is selfless and wants the best for everyone else. Today, 'stranger danger' is ever present in our society, and in this story—with an invitation for the children to write the end—Anjali accepts a lift in a car.

The lift

I'm nine, and I've got lots of things to carry to school because I'm making cakes at after-school club tonight. I've got my cooking tin, my book bag, my lunch box and my trainers, and my arms feel like they're being stretched as I try to carry all those things.

We've got PE today. I don't like PE. We have to run round the playground three times before we start, and Jeremy Petrie always laughs at the way I run.

I'm walking to school on my own as well. I usually call for Julie, but her mum phoned while I was eating my breakfast and Julie's been sick all night so she's staying in bed.

A blue car's pulling up next to me. It's that lady who works at the corner shop where they sell cheese and cold meat. Mum bought some ham from her last Saturday. We had it for tea with a load of chips and a fried egg.

'Hello, Anjali,' she says. She has wound the window down and is smiling at me. 'You look like you're struggling with all those bags. Do you want a lift? Your mum won't mind you getting in the car with me because we know each other, and it's going to rain soon.'

When I was very little—that's ages ago—Mum told me I was never to go with anyone unless they told me it was their birthday next week. Jan did that once. She lives next door to us, and Mum was late home from work and asked Jan to pick me up from school when I thought Mum was going to be there.

'It's my birthday next week,' Jan said to me. Then I knew it

was all right to go with her. But that was ages ago and I don't need to bother with that now.

The lady's got out of her car. She's wearing a white jumper and high-heeled shoes. She's opening the back door and putting my bags on the back seat and helping me get in. Now she's closing the door and going back to the driver's seat.

'Are you going to work?' I ask her.

'Later,' she says, catching my eye in the mirror. Later. She is smiling in the mirror—at me, I think. I smile back.

The car is turning left. It'll go right next, then we're at school. It'll only take two minutes. There's Sam. He's in my class at school. I wave at him. He nods back. He's carrying his cooking things as well.

'Don't wave,' the lady says. 'It's silly.'

She's driven past the end of the road where school is. She should have turned right. We're going towards the railway station now.

'You've missed the turn,' I say.

'I've got to fetch something from my house. You're early for school, what with me giving you a lift. What time do you have to be there?'

'Ten to nine,' I reply. She squints at her watch.

'Plenty of time,' she says.

I lift my hand and fiddle with the handle on the door. It doesn't move. A surge of energy rushes up to my face. I want to get out. I don't feel safe. I am trapped in a car with someone I don't really know, and I'm not quite sure where we're going.

❖

There are two endings to this story. In the first one, Anjali escapes when the woman stops the car at traffic lights—she winds the window down and starts shouting for help.

In the second ending, an advert appears in a shop window asking if anyone has seen a girl carrying a book bag, a tin with cooking things in, a lunch box and a pair of trainers.

What are your feelings about this story?

Other children have said...

'...it's sad because when children get kidnapped you don't often hear they escape... Anjali didn't know what was happening to her...'

'...you should never get in a car, even if you know the person...'

Other things children have said

'...you must always know who's picking you up...'

'...not all strangers want to hurt you. Some of them are kind, but you mustn't trust them...'

Thinking time

- How can you keep yourself really safe?
- Make a list of people you can completely trust. Why do you trust them?

Prayer

Dear God, you know when someone is hurting or not feeling safe. Help us to keep ourselves as safe as possible all the time. Amen

Thinking time activity

Write the two endings to the story, either from the child's point of view or through the eyes of a narrator. Make a list of rules for keeping yourself really safe.

Living with separated parents

Parents, don't be hard on your children.
Raise them properly. Teach them and instruct
them about the Lord.

Ephesians 6:4

Love is more important than anything else.
It is what ties everything completely together.

Colossians 3:14

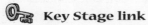

Key Stage link

KS2: 4c: To be aware of different types of relationship, including marriage and those between families and friends, and to develop the skills to be effective in relationships—in this case, with separated parents.

Bible link

The Bible places great importance on the family unit for support and love. Many children have to develop the skill of coping with parents who live in different houses. This story, which looks at this particular situation, would be especially appropriate in December as it raises issues about celebrating Christmas when parents are living apart, as well as the reasons for the Christian festival.

Aeroplane angel and the advert candle

Hayley's dad works at the hospital and lives in a house near the football ground. Hayley's mum works in a school and lives in a flat near the petrol station. And Hayley? She sees her dad every other weekend. 'I'll pick her up at eight o'clock tomorrow night,' Mum says. Dad smiles and nods his head. At least they don't argue like they used to.

Other children have said...

'...you don't really know what they're arguing about and they go on and on and on...'

'...you get scared, especially when they start shouting and swearing...'

'...all sorts of worries go through your head. My aunt and uncle argued and we didn't see them for years...'

'...it could lead to them falling out for ever...'

'Stick your bag in the front room,' Dad says, 'then we'll go. We're going to buy a Christmas tree.' There is a twinkle in his eye. That means they will be doing something else as well.

Dad's dilapidated Fiesta is overtaken by a dark green sports car as they drive down the dual-carriageway.

'He might have a sports car, but he's not going where we're going,' Dad laughs.

'Where are we going, then?'

'I've told you. We're buying a Christmas tree.' Dad winks. There's more to this than meets the eye.

❖

They drive for half an hour, chatting all the time. The engine of a small aeroplane buzzes overhead.

'See that plane,' Dad says. 'That'll be us in a few minutes.'

His grin is so big, his gums are showing. Hayley's stomach tries to tie itself into a knot.

'W… w… we're going up in one of those tiny little planes to buy a Christmas tree?' she stammers.

'Yup!' Her stomach pulls the knot tight as Dad turns into a little road which leads to a flying club.

A short man with a slight limp walks towards them as Dad parks the car.

'There's John,' Dad says, and waves. 'He's a friend of mine at the hospital and flies planes for a hobby.' Hayley has never heard Dad talk about John before, but he is grinning at her.

'Ready for a spin, then?' he says. 'I've done all the checks and we're ready to go.'

It must be safe if Dad's going up as well, Hayley thinks.

'Here's where the Piper Warriors are all parked,' John tells them as they walk behind a row of five planes. 'You can fit two adults in the front, one child and one Christmas tree in the back.'

He helps Hayley climb on to the wing, slide into the back, fasten the seatbelt and plug in her headphones. She is not sure if she feels sick with fear or excitement. Dad and John strap themselves in the front.

'Clear prop!' John shouts, and the plane shudders as the engine surges into life. The control tower clears them and they taxi on to the runway—faster, faster, up, up, lurching and bumping. They're up, off the ground, and she can see someone walking across a field and a dog racing ahead. And there's a house with a blue cover over its swimming-pool, and cars travelling slowly along a main road. She is so small in this enormous clear blue sky. Is this what a bird feels like?

They land 25 minutes later.

'Enjoy that?' John asks.

'It was brilliant!' is all she can say. 'Dead wicked!'

'And the Christmas trees,' John laughs, 'are in the garden centre across the road from the airfield.'

They choose a small tree—it has to be small or it won't fit in the plane—some decorations and a new set of fairy lights. Hayley spots an angel with shining gold and silver wings. It is half-price because the left wing is damaged.

'Can we get this for the top of the tree?' she begs. 'We can mend it with glue and she'll be all right in the plane because she's used to flying.'

'She'll be an aeroplane angel, then,' Dad says, 'who eats apples and... amazing artichokes at... afternoon tea.'

Hayley laughs. Her dad is funny sometimes.

'You've spent 40 pounds 55p,' the lady at the counter tells them, 'so you get a free Advent candle. I'll slip it in the bag for you.'

It is a squash in the back of the plane. The tree branches wave and bounce as the plane cuts through the air. Aeroplane angel is perched on Hayley's arm, watching the shadows the fences and trees make as the plane rises above them.

Do real angels have flying lessons? Hayley suddenly wonders. Do they get hungry?

Do they enjoy scaring people like they did after baby Jesus was born? Do they get injured if they do a crash landing? She looks at aeroplane angel, who looks back at her but says nothing.

Hayley enjoys the flight back to the club airport. Her tummy does not feel as tight and her heart does not beat as fast. John says 'goodbye' to them and walks towards his BMW.

'We'll decorate the tree when we get home,' Dad says as they get back in the Fiesta.

Hayley and Mum decorated their tree last week. Dad's will be different, though, because aeroplane angel will be at the top.

What would be the good things about having two homes?

Other children have said...

'...more space...'

'...two lifestyles....'

'...each parent would spoil you...'

'...there is no good...'

'...you have to keep moving and you wouldn't know where you were. It'd be very confusing...'

'...you need to see your parents together...'

'...I'd lose things and forget things, then I'd get told off even more...'

They stop off for burgers and chips and then the supermarket to buy Dad some food for next week. It is five o'clock by the time they get home. An hour later, aeroplane angel is perched on top of the Christmas tree.

'Can we open our presents?' Hayley asks.

'It's not Christmas Day yet!' Dad says.

'I know, but you're working at your smelly old hospital on Christmas Day, so I won't see you. Please!'

She makes him open the ones she has brought for him first—the calendar she made at school and a new tie she saved up for. He is admiring the tie when all the lights go out—the Christmas tree lights, the hall light, the main light, the street lights. The fridge-freezer in the kitchen stops whirring as well.

'Whooooh!' Dad says. 'That's a power cut. Where's that Advent candle? Good thing we spent so much money this morning.'

'It's by the glue on the table, I think.'

Dad feels his way into the kitchen and searches for some matches. Gentle light flickers on the walls as he returns. Carefully he melts the bottom of the candle, sets it on a plate and lights the wick at the top, making shadows dance on his face.

'We had an Advent candle at school when I was in year 3,' Hayley giggles. 'I thought it was an advert candle.'

'Advert?'

'Like they have on the telly.'

'You are funny!' Dad says.

'Well, they didn't have tellies when Jesus was born, but they did have things like candles, so I thought that was what it was for. Dad, do angels have flying lessons before they're sent to go and scare people?'

'Hayley, I can't keep up with you! I've no idea, but I'll tell you something they didn't have when Jesus was born.'

'What?'

'They didn't have decorations or cards or Christmas trees or presents.'

Hayley's present is still under the tree. She picks it up and grapples with the sticky tape and paper until a box slips out. Carefully she opens it.

Inside is a silver necklace with a single pearl.

'I wanted to give you something special,' Dad says. 'Something that will last.'

She undoes the clasp and lays the necklace round her neck. She does not need a mirror to know how beautiful it looks. Dad's jumper is soft against her cheek as she gives him a hug.

'Thank you,' she says. 'It's lovely.' At that moment the lights come back on, the fridge-freezer starts whirring and the Christmas tree lights twinkle once more.

'Shall I blow the advert candle out then?' Hayley asks. Dad smiles.

'Leave it burning,' he says. 'Remind ourselves that Christmas is nearly here.'

'Aeroplane angel could fly round the world and do an advert for Christmas now her wing's mended,' Hayley says. 'Tell everyone to get ready.'

'And would you like to fly with her?'

'Of course!'

'And what would you tell everyone? It would have to be about what's special about Christmas.'

Hayley whispers something in her dad's ear.

'I like that,' he whispers back.

What do you think Hayley would tell the world if she was advertising Christmas?

Other children have said...

'...look after people you love...'

'...peace...'

'...it was between her and her dad so we'll never find out...'

'...families are special...'

'...families need looking after...'

What are the best presents people give each other?

Other children have said...

'...anything where a lot of thought has gone into it...'

'...lots of love, all the year round...'

'...presents in boxes, but love is best...'

Other things children have said

'...you don't always get on with the rest of your family, but you have to try to...'

'...my dad and my mum fight, but they don't split up...'

'...my brother and I fight and Mum shouts at us to stop. I like him some of the time...'

Thinking time

- What promises do people make to each other when they get married? What do they actually mean?
- What is the worst thing when parents decide they don't want to live together any more?

Dear God, mums and dads sometimes argue.
Help me to be really strong if I hear them, and
help them calm down and sort out what they're
arguing about. Amen

Thinking time activity

Make a list of things you like doing with
your family and then with your friends.
Are there things that are in both lists?
Would you like to add something
that isn't there at the moment? If
you were going to get married
tomorrow, what would you want
your partner to be like? What
might he or she want you to
be like?

* * * * * * *

Stories to make you think

Written especially for all those working or living with 6–10 year olds who find themselves needing to talk through topical and often sensitive issues, such as bereavement, bullying, family matters, spiritual awareness and self-value. Designed to stimulate discussion between adult and child, the stories are based mainly on real-life experiences and use biblical insights and thinking time to provide an accessible entry point into difficult subjects.

REF 1 84101 034 0, £3.99

* * * * * * *

More stories to make you think

Following on from the popular *Stories to Make You Think*, this book provides a further selection of topical and often sensitive subjects designed to stimulate discussion between adult and child. The author uses biblical insights and thinking time to provide an accessible entry point into diffcult subjects. Each story has been researched and tested in Circle Time and PSHE at primary level and can be used either in a one-to-one situation or with a group in the classroom, church or family.

REF 1 84101 141 X, £4.99